where are you going ?

to my granny's

oh no you're not

why?

dinner is served!

what's to eat?

some joooosey red meat !!!

gosh! what big
ears you've got!

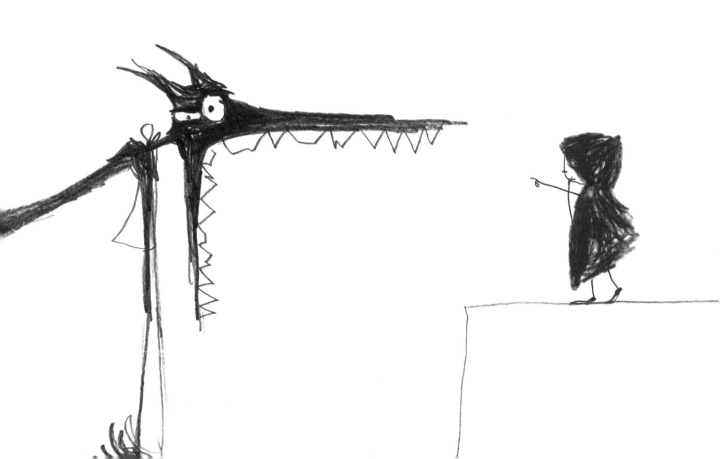

all the better to hear you with ...

you're ever so hairy

Wow, big eyes too

and those are seriously big teeth

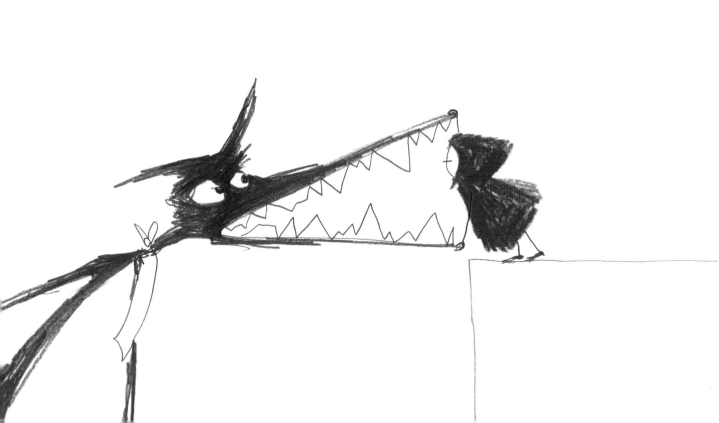

all the better to eat
you with !///

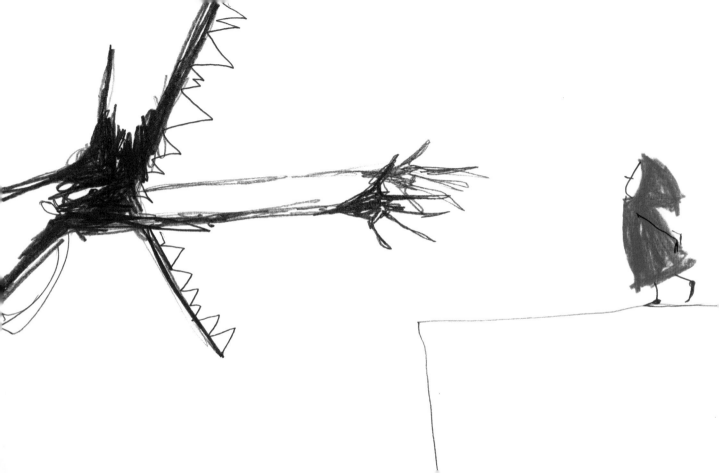

no

no ?

you've got stinky breath

have a sweet

swallow

arrrgh !

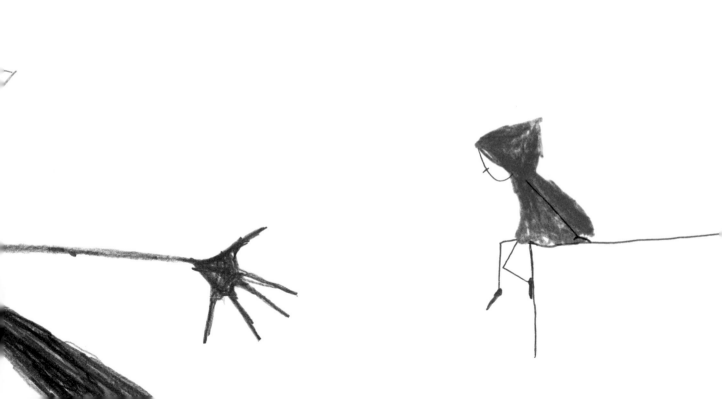